Little Mouse and his dad went around the farm.

I0820458

Little Mouse spotted a rooster.

I am afraid of
its sharp feet and
loud yelling.

Then, Little Mouse spotted a cat.

It has a soft coat
and a big grin.

Sh! Looks can lie,
Little Mouse.

The rooster is harmless and feeds on grain.

But a cat will catch a mouse for its dinner!

Teachers and parents

An important part of becoming a confident, fluent reader is a student's ability to understand what they are reading. Below are some suggestions on how to develop a student's reading comprehension. Make reading this book a shared experience between you and the student. Try to avoid leaving it until the whole book is read before talking about it. Occasionally stop at various intervals throughout the book.

- Ask questions about the characters, the setting, and the meaning;
- Encourage the student to think about what might happen next. It does not matter if the answer is right or wrong, so long as the suggestion makes sense and demonstrates understanding;
- Relate what is happening in the book to any real-life experiences the student may have;
- Pick out any vocabulary that may be new to the student and ask what they think it means. If they don't know, explain it and relate it to what is happening in the book;
- Encourage the student to summarize, in their own words, what they have read.

About this folktale

The Cat and the Rooster is based on a fable called The Cat, the Rooster, and the Young Mouse. It is one of the Aesop's fables from ancient Greece.

What's in the book?

- What animal is the little mouse afraid of?
- What animal is the little mouse's dad afraid of?
- Who has a soft coat and a big grin?

What do you think?

- What animals are you afraid of?
- Should mice be afraid of cats? Why (not)?

Folktales

Jolly Phonics Readers are fully decodable books for new readers.

These Readers have been written with a **carefully controlled vocabulary**, and are specifically designed for students who are learning to read and write with Jolly Phonics.

- The text in these Red Level Books (first level) uses only **decodable regular words** (words that are made up from the 42 letter sounds taught in the first stage of Jolly Phonics) and a small number of **tricky words** (frequently used words that are not fully decodable at this stage).
- All of the tricky words and letter sounds used in this book are shown on the front inside cover. These can be used as a quick practice activity before starting the book.
- **Faint type** is used for silent letters, like the ‹b› in *lamb*.
- **Comprehension questions** and discussion topics are included at the end of the book. These ensure that students are not only able to read the text, but also get meaning from it.

Red Level Readers

Level 0 | Level 1 | Level 2 | Level 3 | Level 4 | Level 5

Folktales

The Cap Seller
Rock Broth
Fox Tricks Panther
The Cat and the Rooster
The Moon on the Millpond
The King's Cheese

MIX
Paper | Supporting responsible forestry
FSC® C016973

© Jolly Learning Ltd 2024 (text) Written by Emily Guille-Marrett
© Anastasiia Bielik 2024 (illustrations) (Beehive Illustration)

ISBN 978-1-83582-142-8

82 Winter Sport Lane, Williston, VT 05495, USA. Tel: +1-800-488-2665
77 Hornbeam Road, Buckhurst Hill, Essex, IG9 6JX, UK. Tel: +44 20 8501 0405

Printed in China. All rights reserved.

www.jollylearning.com info@jollylearning.co.uk

Reference: JL1428
American English Edition

The Moon on the Millpond

in print letters

Folktales

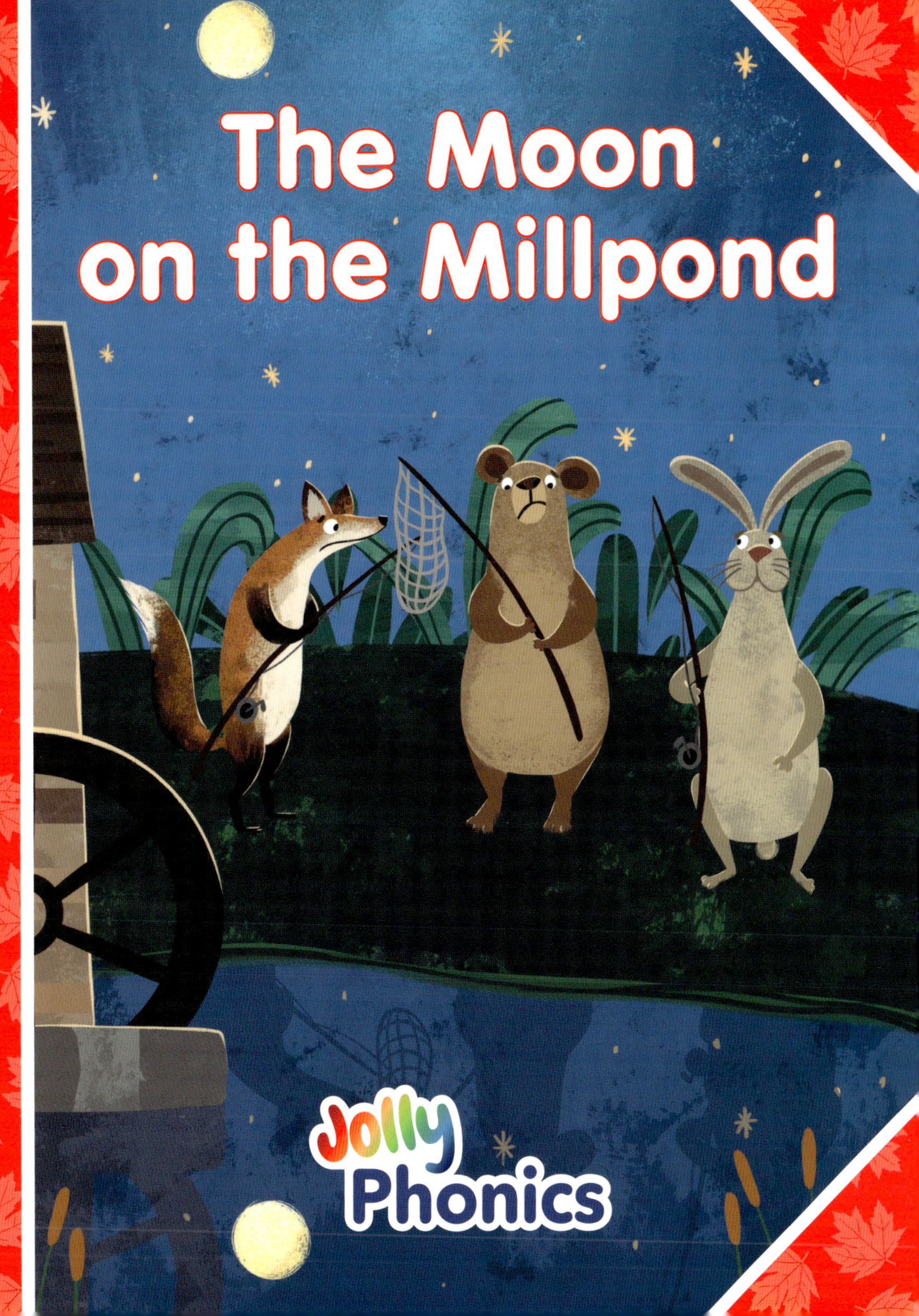

Teachers and parents

Before tackling these Red Level Readers, a student will need to be able to:

- Recognize the basic 42 letter sounds shown in the leaves below;
- Read (blend) regular words containing these letter sounds;
- Recognize the tricky words shown in the flowers below.

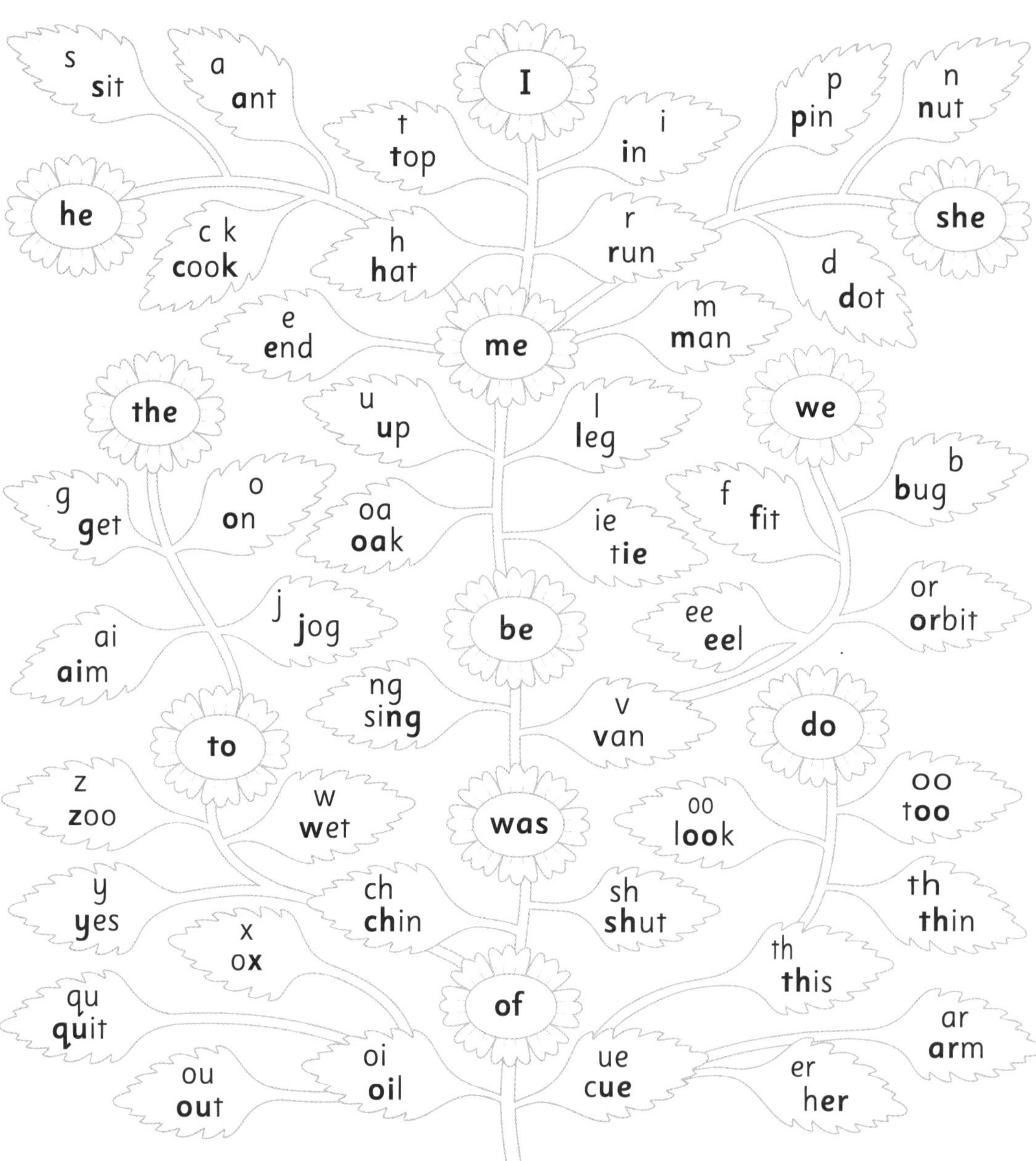